By **Christy Webster** · Illustrated by **Steph Laberis**

grumpycats.com
randomhousekids.com
Educators and librarians, for a variety of teaching tools, visit us at RHTeachersLibrarians.com
ISBN 978-1-5247-6969-7 (trade)—ISBN 978-1-5247-6970-3 (ebook)
Printed in the United States of America
10 9 8 7 6 5 4 3 2 1

Grumpy Cat

GRUMPY CAT'S FIRST WORST CHRISTMAS

A GOLDEN BOOK · NEW YORK

"It's almost time for Christmas, Grumpy Cat!
'Tis the season to be jolly!"

NOEL

Stockings

Lights

"'Tis the season to leave me alone."

"Look, Grumpy Cat! It's snowing!

Let it snow, let it snow—"

"Let it *stop.*"

"But, Grumpy, in the winter we can build
a snow-cat."

"If I have to, mine will have a frown."

"Grumpy Cat, Grumpy Cat, Grumpy Cat,
let's go! Let's sled down this snow!"

"I'd rather live in my wonderland of
NO."

"O Grumpy Cat, O Grumpy Cat, how about we decorate the Christmas tree?"

"I think that thing has termites. This is the *most* terrible time of the year."

"It's time to wrap the presents, Grumpy Cat!"

"Did you say it's time to *rip* the presents?"

"Christmas carolers are here, Grumpy Cat!"

"Jingle bells, jingle bells!"

"Fa la la la la . . . la la la la!"

"How about silent night . . .
all are gone . . . ?
That feels more right."

"We can make cookies for Santa, Grumpy Cat.
And leave a special note."

"Dear **Santa**,
all I want for Christmas . . .
is for it to be over."

"Let's make the fireplace roar!
Grumpy Cat, it's cold outside."

NO

EL

DEAR SANTA,
ALL I WANT FOR
CHRISTMAS IS
FOR IT TO
BE OVER.

"The answer is . . . NO.
I sat by a fireplace once.
It was awful."

"Isn't there anything you like about
Christmas, Grumpy Cat?"

"Well . . . there *are* more things around here to break."

"Uh-oh, Grumpy Cat.
You might be on Santa's naughty list."